Awesome Adventures

PLANES144748

Code is valid for your Wings Around the Globe ebook
and may be redeemed through the Disney Story Central app
on the App Store. Content subject to availability.
Parent permission required.
Code expires on December 31, 2019.

PaRragon

Bath · New York · Cologne · Melbourne · Delhi
Hong Kong · Shenzhen · Singapore · Amsterdam

This edition published by Parragon Books Ltd in 2016 and distributed by

Parragon Inc.
440 Park Avenue South, 13th Floor
New York, NY 10016
www.parragon.com

ISBN 978-1-4748-2132-2

Printed in China

Lightning McQueen dreams of winning the Piston Cup,
but first he needs to win the final race in California.

Lightning's loyal driver, Mack, is exhausted, but Lightning
forces him to drive to California so they can arrive early.

Suddenly, a group of street racers drive up alongside
Mack and try to bump him off the road.

Mack swerves across the road, and Lightning rolls out of the truck!

Lightning tries to make his own way to California, but he drives too fast and crashes on his way into the sleepy town of Radiator Springs.

Sheriff is furious that Lightning has destroyed the road—and gotten caught in a telephone wire.

The town lawyer, Sally, says that Lightning
should stay and fix the damaged road.

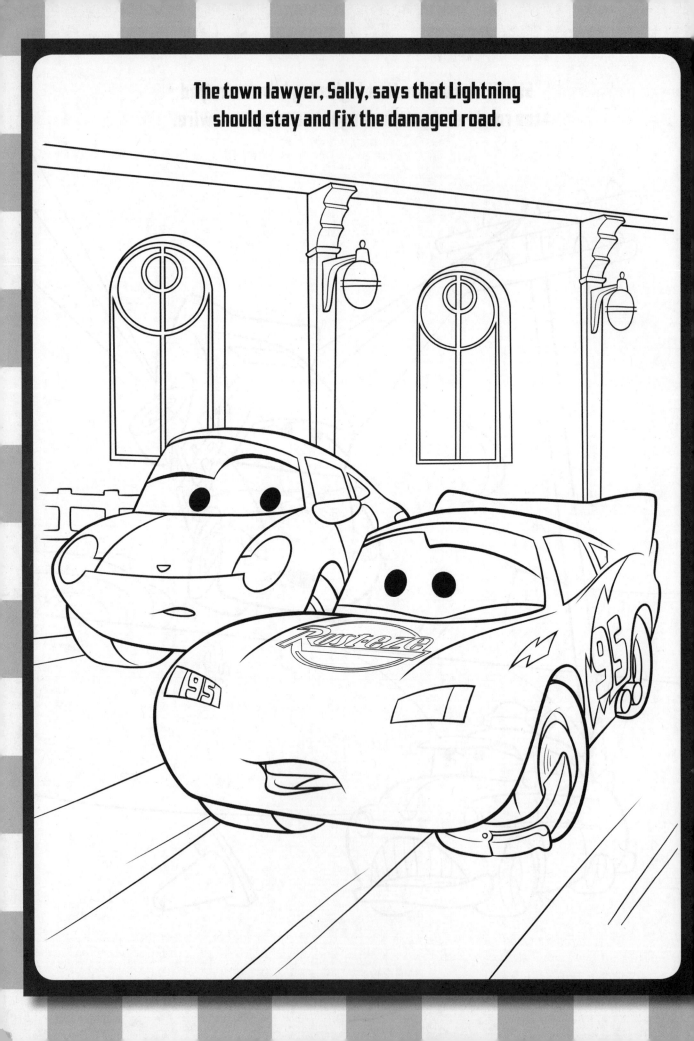

Lightning has to tow Bessie to fix the road.
He thinks he is too good for this—he is a race car, after all!

Doc Hudson is an old racing champion. Doc watches Lightning to make sure he fixes the road properly.

Doc challenges Lightning to a race in the desert.
If Lightning wins, he can leave Radiator Springs.

Lightning loses control after a tight turn and ends up in a cactus patch.
The town's tow truck, Mater, has to pull Lightning free.

Later, Lightning discovers that Doc once won a Piston Cup!
Lightning tells everyone in town.

Sally takes Lightning on a tour of Radiator Springs.
She tells him how busy and popular the town used to be.

Lightning wants to learn from Doc, but Doc doesn't want to talk about racing.
Instead, he tells Lightning about the crash that ended his career.

Everyone in Radiator Springs loves the smooth new road.
It makes the whole town feel new again!

Lightning starts to make friends with everyone in Radiator Springs.
He spends a lot of time with Sally. The whole town spruces itself up!

One day, Mack arrives in town—he's been looking for Lightning. Mack says they have to leave now if they want to make it to the Final Piston Cup race.

News reporters arrive in Radiator Springs. Lightning tells Sally he has to leave and sadly asks Mack to take him to the Piston Cup race.

Lightning arrives in California. He feels sad about leaving his friends behind in Radiator Springs.

Then, surprise! Doc and the rest of the gang have
come to the race to cheer on Lightning!

During the race, The King, a famous race car, crashes but Lightning helps him across the line. Lightning loses the race, but he knows he did the right thing.

After the race, Lightning returns to Radiator Springs. The whole town has been given a new lease on life. Everyone is very excited!

Thanks to his new friends, Lightning has learned that life is not just about being fast, but also about slowing down to enjoy things.

Mater is waiting for his best friend, Lightning McQueen, who has just won the Hudson Hornet Memorial Piston Cup!

On a TV show, Italian race car Francesco Bernoulli claims he is much faster than Lightning. Mater calls in to defend his friend.

Lightning is determined to beat Francesco in the World Grand Prix.
Mater and Lightning travel to Japan for the first race.

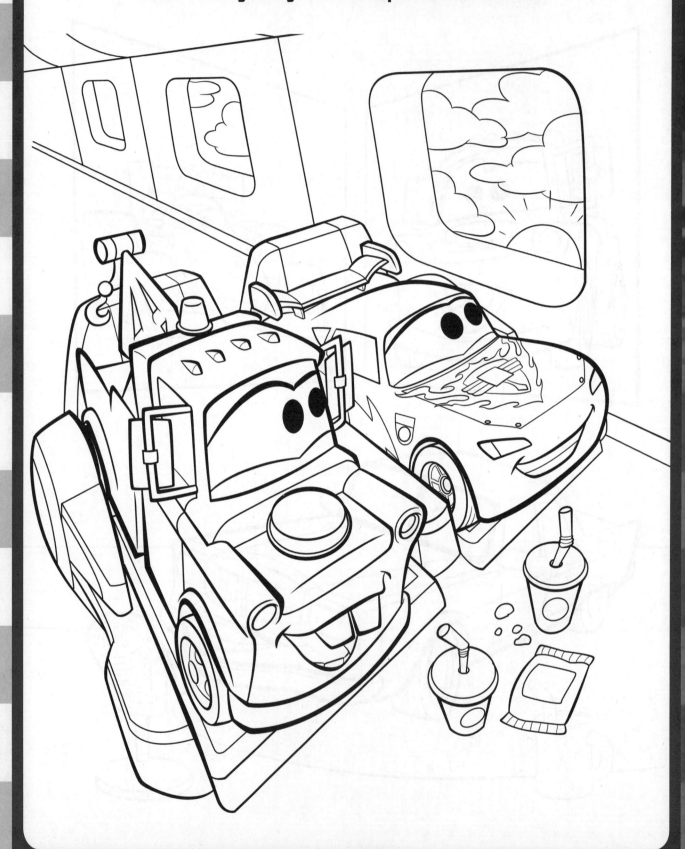

Finn McMissile is a British secret agent. His mission is to spy on the wicked Professor Z, who is developing a secret weapon with a mysterious master criminal.

Finn meets fellow agent Holley Shiftwell in Japan. They are supposed to meet with an American agent who has some information for them.

Finn and Holley think Mater is the American agent. When Holley makes plans to meet with Mater after the first race, Mater thinks she wants a date!

During the race, Mater hears Holley in his
headset and sets off to meet her.

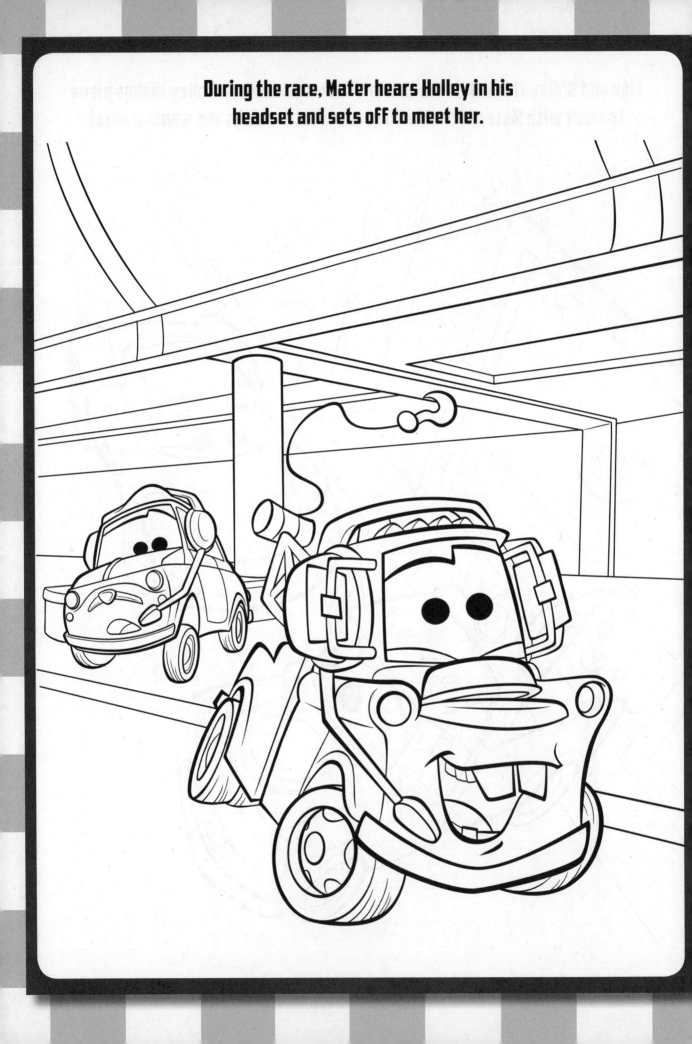

But Lightning thinks his friend is giving him racing tips and swerves all over the track!

Holley's directions lead Mater to Finn, who is fighting off some of the bad guys. Mater thinks it's some kind of karate demonstration!

Lightning lost the race to Francesco Bernoulli.
Lightning is angry and blames Mater, who decides to go home.

Finn follows Mater to the airport to protect him
from the bad guys who work for Professor Z.

Siddeley, the spy plane, swoops down to rescue Finn and Mater.

Holley is already on board the plane. She finds the information the American agent planted on Mater—it's a picture of an engine. They decide to go to the next World Grand Prix race.

The second World Grand Prix race is in Italy. Lightning admits to Francesco that he really misses Mater, before going on to win the race.

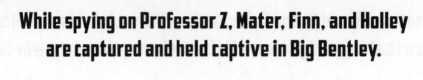

While spying on Professor Z, Mater, Finn, and Holley are captured and held captive in Big Bentley.

They quickly escape and set off to the final race in London.
Lightning is excited to see his friend again, but Mater realizes
the bad guys have planted a bomb on him!

Suddenly, Mater realizes who the master criminal is! Mater uses the jet engines
Holley gave him to fly to Buckingham Palace—with Lightning in tow.

Sir Miles Axlerod, the creator of the World Grand Prix, is at Buckingham Palace.

Mater approaches the Queen and explains that Professor Z and Axlerod have been working together. Axlerod is the master criminal!

Because of his heroic service, the Queen knights Mater. Then he and Lightning return to Radiator Springs—the best of friends again!

Dusty Crophopper is a small-town crop dusting plane. He dreams of racing in the Wings Around The Globe Rally against the fastest planes in the world.

Skipper used to fly for the Navy. Even though he doesn't fly anymore, Skipper helps Dusty train for the rally.

Dusty enters the qualifying race for the rally, but he gets off to a bad start when his crop sprayer accidentally turns on!

Dusty fails to qualify for the rally. He is sad and disappointed.
Even his friends, Dottie and Chug, can't cheer him up.

One day, a race official comes to Dusty's hometown of Propwash Junction to give him some good news—he can be in the rally after all!

Dusty flies to New York for the start of the race. He is very excited to be a part of it, but he is too shy to talk to the other planes.

**Dusty meets Mexican racing champion El Chupacabra.
Dusty is a big fan of El Chu. The two become instant friends.**

While the other racers fly high, Dusty stays low. He is afraid of heights!

The first stage of the rally takes the racers across the Atlantic Ocean. Dusty flies through a freezing hailstorm and nearly crashes into an iceberg!

In Germany, Dusty and El Chu meet Franz, a little car who can turn into a plane called Von Fliegenhosen.

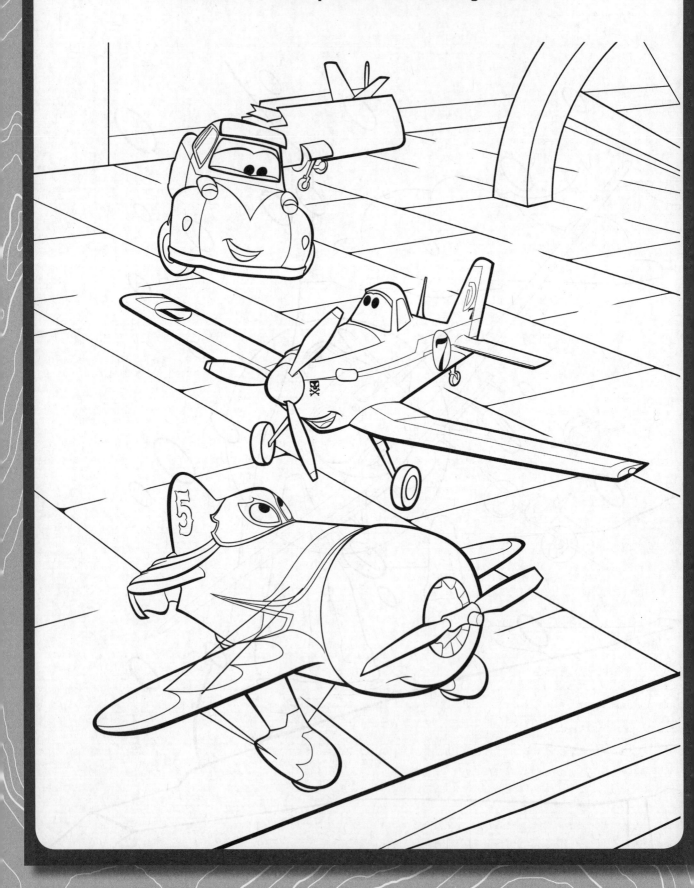

Von Fliegenhosen has a great idea! If Dusty takes off his crop sprayer, he can fly much faster.

In the next race, the planes have to fly low through the mountains in India. Dusty quickly passes the other racers and moves up the leader board.

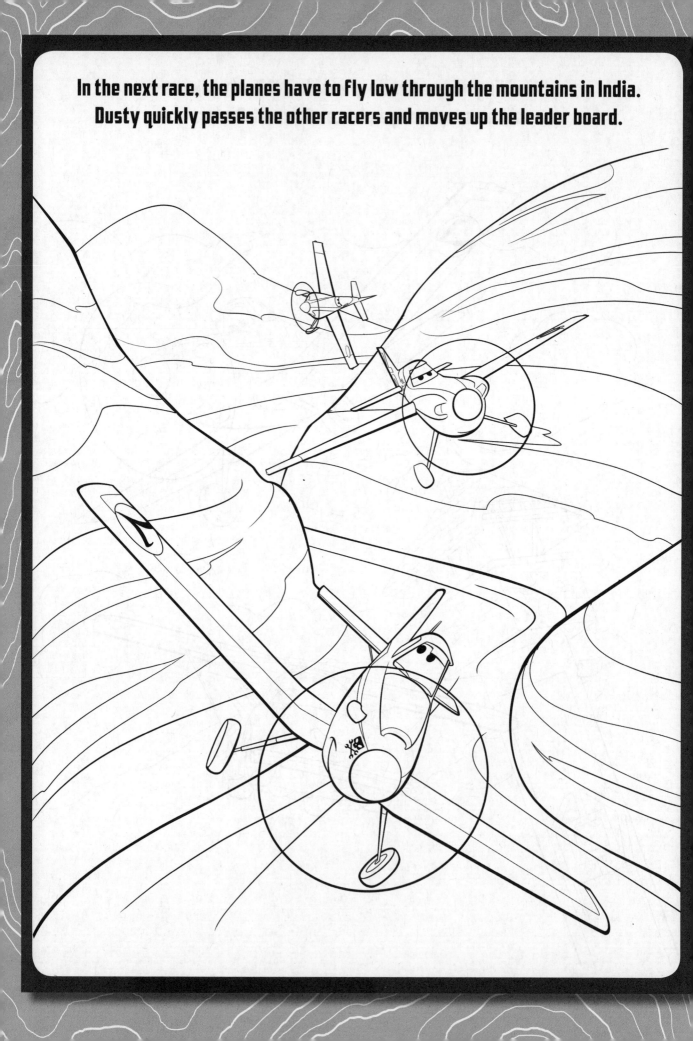

Ripslinger, a three-time rally champion, is angry at all the attention Dusty is getting. He is supposed to be the star of the rally!

**The next leg of the rally takes the planes to Nepal.
When Dusty lands he is in first place!**

Dusty's friends in Propwash Junction call to congratulate him.
Seeing Dusty chase his dream makes Skipper wish he could fly again.

Dusty has become the star of the rally! He has millions of fans
from all over the world who cheer for him.

On his way to Mexico, Dusty is damaged in a storm. The other racers give Dusty their spare parts. Now he can finish the rally!

The final stage of the race is from Mexico to New York.
Dusty is determined to win.

Ripslinger is worried that Dusty is going to beat him, so he sends his sidekicks, Ned and Zed, after Dusty to stop him in the Deadstick Desert.

**Suddenly, Skipper comes roaring into view and saves Dusty.
Dusty can't believe Skipper is flying again!**

Dusty realizes that he must face his fear of heights if he wants to fly faster and catch up to Ripslinger. Dusty zooms off, soaring high above the clouds.

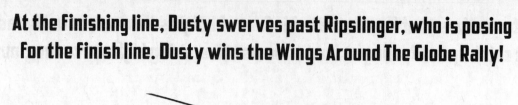

At the finishing line, Dusty swerves past Ripslinger, who is posing for the finish line. Dusty wins the Wings Around The Globe Rally!

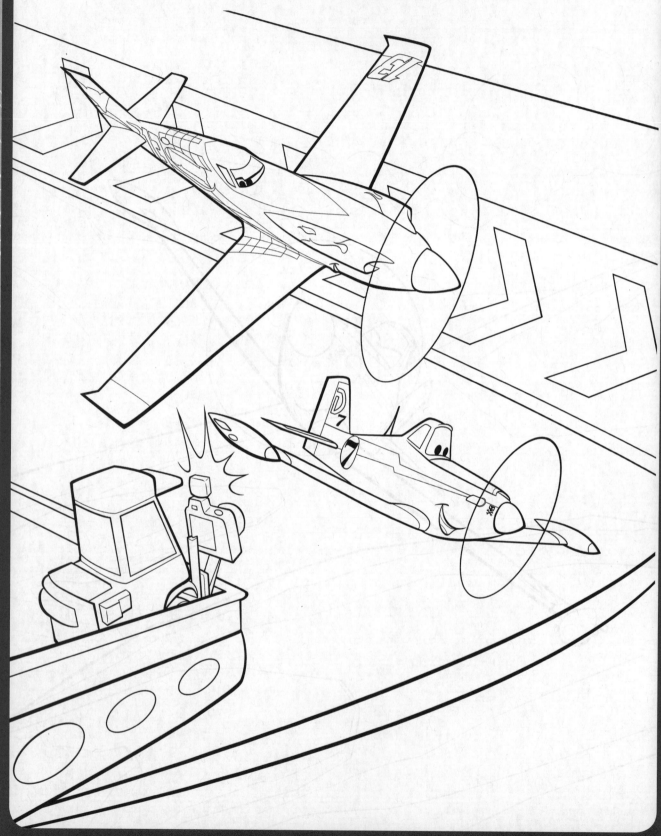

One day, champion racer Dusty Crophopper is out flying with his trainer, Skipper. Suddenly, something goes wrong with Dusty's engine! But he manages to land safely.

Dottie the mechanic tells Dusty his gearbox is damaged.
He won't be able to race anymore. If he pushes himself too hard,
a red light will flash on his control panel to warn him.

**Dusty wants to prove he is still a racer, but he flies too fast
and crashes into the gas station, starting a big fire!**

Mayday, Propwash's old Fire engine, can't put out the blaze—his hoses are leaking!
He and Dusty pull over the water tower to put out the Flames.

Two safety officials close down the airfield. It cannot reopen until Mayday is updated and the town hires a second firefighter.

Mayday tells Dusty that planes used to help put out fires by dropping water from above. Dusty volunteers to be the town's second firefighter!

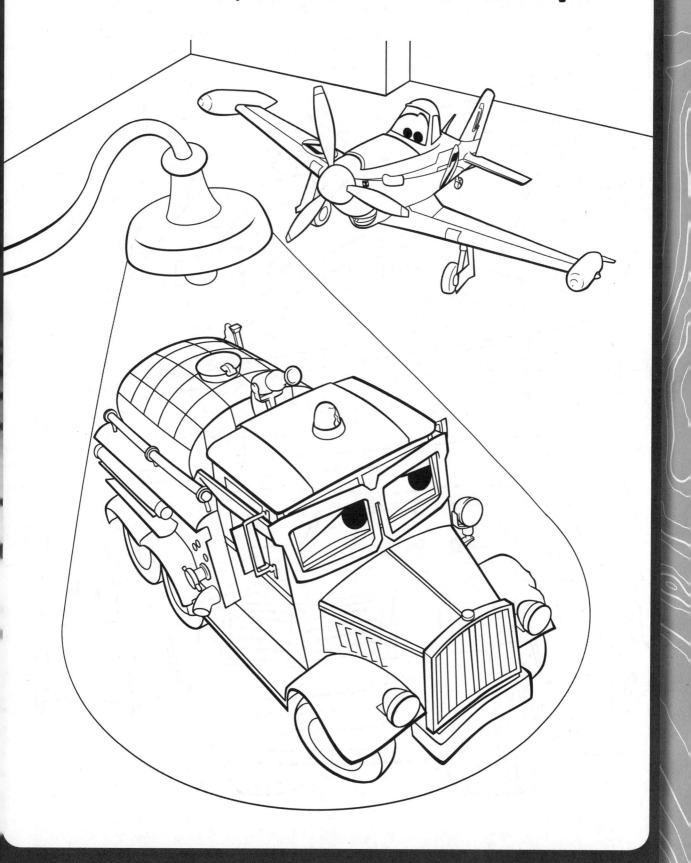

Dusty flies to the nearby Piston Peak National Park for training. He meets Cad Spinner, the Superintendent of the park and owner of the Fusel Lodge hotel.

**Suddenly the alarm sounds! There's a fire in the park!
Fire Chief Blade Ranger flies above the flames.**

Dusty flies up to get a better view. He sees Dipper,
a super-scooper, dropping retardant on the blaze.

When they land, Blade is angry with Dusty for getting in the way. Blade doesn't care that Dusty is a champion racer.

Dusty is equipped with pontoons so he can scoop up water.
He starts training with Blade, but he can't fly fast
enough and his warning light flashes red.

Dusty struggles with training. He finds it especially hard learning the right moment to drop retardant.

A few days later, it is the grand reopening of the Fusel Lodge. But as everyone celebrates, the alarm sounds and the team takes off to fight the fire.

Dusty's engine stalls as he tries to refill his pontoons.
He's stuck in the rapids, drifting toward a waterfall!

Blade swoops in and rescues Dusty just as he is about to drop over the cliff.

But Blade gets damaged by the intense heat of the fire,
so Windlifter carries him back to base.

Cad refuses to evacuate the Lodge on opening night. Desperate to protect it, he diverts the firefighters' water to the roof sprinklers.

Flaming debris blocks the railroad line and the road out of Piston Peak, leaving cars stranded.

Dusty flies as fast as he can to help with the rescue.
He puts out the fire just as his warning light starts to flash red.

Dusty has pushed himself too far. His engines start to fail and he crashes through the treetops, toward the ground.

Days later, Dusty wakes up in his hangar. Maru, the air-attack team's mechanic, has fixed Dusty and built him a new gearbox. Dusty can race again!

Blade tells Dusty that he is now a certified firefighter and thanks him for his help.

Dottie has fixed Mayday—he's as good as new! With Mayday's makeover and Dusty's certification, the Propwash Junction Fire Department has never been better!